I Died Here

GEORGE SHEA

 A PACEMAKER BESTELLERS® BOOK

FEARON PITMAN PUBLISHERS, INC.
Belmont, California

The PACEMAKER BESTELLERS®

Bestellers® I

Diamonds in the Dirt
Night of the Kachina
The Verlaine Crossing
Silvabamba
The Money Game

Flight to Fear
The Time Trap
The Candy Man
Three Mile House
Dream of the Dead

Bestellers® II

Black Beach
Crash Dive
Wind Over Stonehenge
Gypsy
Escape from Tomorrow

The Demeter Star
North to Oak Island
So Wild a Dream
Wet Fire
Tiger, Lion, Hawk

Bestellers® III

Star Gold
Bad Moon
Jungle Jenny
Secret Spy
Little Big Top

The Animals
Counterfeit!
Night of Fire and Blood
Village of Vampires
I Died Here

Series director: Robert G. Bander

Designer: Richard Kharibian

Cover designer and illustrator: Bill Shields

ISBN-0-8224-5364-9

Library of Congress Catalog Card Number: 78-72329

Printed in the United States of America.

1. 9 8 7 6 5 4 3 2 1

CONTENTS

CHAPTER 1
THIS WAY TO DROKOLA

Larry Arkos was afraid. He was driving in a strange country. His car was going at top speed down a winding mountain road. He didn't know how he had gotten there. He knew only that he was in Greece.

It was late in the day, and Larry was lost and tired. He saw a road sign. It said "Drokola." Suddenly he felt fear rising even higher inside him.

Driving past the sign, he went up a winding dirt road. He came to a little town. He drove through the town and then came to a cemetery. He got out of the car and walked to the cemetery gate. He pulled it open and went inside. He sensed that he was looking for something, but he wasn't sure what it was. Then he came to a grave. On the stone above the grave he saw a name—"Nikos Vanos."

NIKOS
VANOS

"That's my name!" he said. His whole body began to shake. He wanted to cry out, "That's my name! That's me in that grave! I *died* here!"

Then, behind him, he heard a sound. Turning, he saw a large black dog coming at him. The dog was coming for his throat. Its teeth bit deep into Larry's arm as he tried to fight it off.

And then Larry was running—running from what? He turned again. Two figures dressed in black were chasing him.

"You died here! You died here! You stay here!" their voices screamed after him. He ran and ran. He couldn't find his way out of the cemetery. He tried to climb an old iron fence. Something hit him from behind and knocked him down.

When he got to his feet, the figures in black were almost upon him. He ran again. Then a hand reached up from a grave. Grabbing him by a leg, it began to pull him down—down into the grave.

Larry woke up—screaming. He looked up and felt the room spin around him. The dream was over.

As he got out of bed, his body shook as it had in the dream. He looked around the little room. He asked himself, "What is this place? Where am I? Why am I here?"

He walked to a window and looked out. The morning light showed that he was in a little town. All the houses were made of stone. They ran up and down the hills that ringed the town. Then, when he looked down into the street, he saw a shop window. A sign in the window said "Drachos Manos."

"Think! Think!" he said out loud. "Where am I? What is this place?" He drove his mind to work, to shake off the dream. Then—he knew.

He was in a small hotel in Kopos, a little town in Greece. He had come there yesterday. The night before, he had been in another small hotel in another Greek town some miles away. That night, he had had the same dream.

I'm losing my mind, he thought to himself. I don't know what I'm doing any more. I've had this same mad dream every night for weeks.

He thought again of the name of the town in his dream—Drokola. *Was* there such a place? He couldn't find it on any map. He had driven all over Greece looking for it. And he had met no one who knew of it.

But it *had* to be there. It all had to mean *something*. The dream always seemed so real. And he knew that sometimes dreams came true.

Suddenly, Larry wished there was a phone in his room so he could call home. He wanted to call Anne and tell her he loved her. Tell her he was coming home.

I've got to get out of here, he thought. I've got to get out of this town—out of this whole country!

He got dressed, went downstairs, and checked out of the hotel. Then he got into his car and started driving.

I'll drive to the nearest big city, he thought to himself. I'll drive to Volos. I can be there by late tonight. Then I'll get on a plane and be home tomorrow.

As he drove, he thought of Anne and home. He began to feel better.

This whole trip was against all reason. It made no sense, he thought to himself. What made me do it? Home was in California, where he had a good job, where he had Anne. There, his life made sense.

But it was in California that the dreams had started. Almost every night, the same dream. He was in Greece. Then he saw that sign—"Drokola." Then he went down the winding road that led to the town and, finally, the cemetery. Then the name on the stone—"Nikos Vanos." The black dog. The hand coming up from the grave.

None of it made sense, but all of it seemed so *real*. Night by night, it tore at his mind. Finally, the dreams drove him here to Greece.

As he thought of the dream, he drove the car faster. He took a wrong turn, then another.

Suddenly, he was lost. It was growing dark, and he was still in the mountains. There were no other cars on the road.

As he drove around a bend in the road, something jumped in front of the car. A dark shape. Was it a person? An animal? He tried to stop before he hit it. He came down hard on the brakes. The car skidded off the road, then came to a stop. He was all right. He looked at the road. He saw nothing there. Nothing.

What had happened? *Had* something jumped out in front of him? Perhaps it had been an animal crossing the road. Perhaps, too, it had all been in his mind. Then, in front of him, he saw it. A road sign. *The* sign. It said "Drokola."

The sign pointed to a winding dirt road—the road in his dream. Suddenly, Larry's heart started pounding. His hands began shaking. "No!" he told himself out loud. "Don't! Don't go down that road! You've come far enough. You've done enough. There's an evil place down that road. You'll *die* there!"

For a long time, he sat and looked at the sign. It called to him. "Drokola!"

I can drive away from here, he thought. I can

go all the way back to America, but it won't make any difference. The dreams and the fear will still be with me. I can't run. I have to face the dream and the fear—now.

Starting up the car, he drove back on the road and past the sign. Then he went down the winding dirt road the sign pointed to. His mouth was dry. He had never been so afraid in his life.

At the end of the road was a town—the same little Greek town that was in his dream. He drove through it, knowing what came next. At the edge of the town was the cemetery.

He stopped the car and got out. It was almost dark as he walked to the cemetery gate. He opened it and went inside.

CHAPTER **2**

THE WOMAN IN BLACK

The old iron gate made a loud noise as it closed behind him. It made him jump. The sky was growing very dark as a cold wind came blowing in from the west.

Under his feet the ground was soft. It seemed to be pulling him down into the earth. He lifted one foot, then the other as he slowly made his way among the stones.

He knew what he was looking for. The names passed before his eyes: Stakatos, Lollos, Skouras, Pappas, Costos. It was like reading a telephone book of the dead. Finally, he came to the last page—the last row of stones. Then, as he knew he would, he found it.

The stone said, "Nikos Vanos." Just like in the dream. The stone was brown and cracked, and it had sunk far into the earth. As Larry looked at the stone, a dog howled in the distance. Wind blew the trees. A group of dark birds made high screaming sounds as it made its way across the sky. Larry felt unable to move. He stood stuck to the spot.

Then he sensed something moving behind him. He knew he had to move—do something—run—strike out. He raised his hand in the air. He turned.

It was a very old woman, dressed in black. She might have been 100 years old. She opened her mouth to speak. Larry saw only a few black teeth.

"I have been waiting for you," she said. "You lived here. You died here."

She spoke Greek, but Larry understood her. His father had been born in Greece and had come to America as a young man. Larry knew Greek almost as well as he knew English.

"Who are you?" he asked her in Greek.

She bent down and placed a dark flower on Nikos Vanos's grave. "You will know," she said. "Come with me."

Turning, the old woman walked slowly back toward the cemetery gate. She went out the gate and walked down the dirt road that led past the cemetery. As she walked, the wind blew her black clothes around her. Still filled with fear, Larry walked a few steps behind her.

Finally, the woman came to a small stone house and went inside. Larry followed her in. The place was almost dark. A small, dying fire in the fireplace gave off the only light.

Larry drew a deep breath. The sights and smells of the place filled him with a strong, strange feeling. Suddenly he sensed that in some unknown way he knew the place. Or that in another time he *had* known it. Had been here. Had lived—and died—here.

Was it possible? No, the idea made no sense. He had been told he had been born in America. And, until now, he had never left America—as far as he knew.

"Sit," the old woman said.

He sat to one side of the fire. She sat across from him, the dying fire burning between them. She looked into his eyes. "Long ago, you lived in this village," she said.

I don't believe her, Larry thought. She's putting me on.

"What was my name?" he asked.

"Your name was Nikos Vanos."

"Nikos Vanos is dead," said Larry. "How long ago did he die?"

"You died 25 years ago tomorrow. When you were a young man." The woman smiled and showed her black teeth. A new chill went through Larry.

"Who are you?" he asked her.

"One who knew you," she said. "One who knows many things. One who knows the truth about your death."

"What is that truth?" Larry asked, feeling fear rising again in his throat.

"You were murdered—murdered because of what you knew."

"How? Who . . . ?"

"I do not know. I know only that the murderer still lives. He is still here in this village. You knew him and believed in him. Then, when your back was turned, he. . . ."

She didn't finish. For a time she sat, saying nothing. Larry felt cold. Was there a man out there in the night, not far away, who may have killed him in another life?

Then, slowly, the old woman rose to her feet. Going to the door, she spoke to Larry. "You want to know more. You must look, ask."

Larry rose and joined her. "Where?" he asked.

She opened the door and pointed to a house on top of a nearby hill.

"In that house," she said. "The last day you were alive, you walked out from that house. Go there now. Go and find the truth."

As he went out the door, Larry turned to her. "Why?" he asked. "Why must I do this?"

The woman laughed, an ugly laugh that caught in her throat. "You will not rest until you find out," she said. "Until you do, you will walk the earth in fear and darkness. You must find the man who. . . ."

She didn't finish. She turned and closed the door, leaving Larry outside.

He started to walk away from the house. It was dark now, dark and cold. The stars were out. Larry looked up at them. He felt a very long way from home. A very long way from anything that made sense. But he knew the old woman was right. He wouldn't, *couldn't* rest until he knew.

He made his way to the house on top of the hill. It was brown and large, old and broken down. Like the little stone house below, something about it made him think he had once known the place. A strange feeling led him to believe he had been there before. He knocked on the front door. After a few moments he heard voices inside. Then the door opened.

CHAPTER **3**

BEHIND THE PICTURE

A woman stood there. She was tall and straight and had white hair.

"Yes?" she asked. Larry looked at her. He saw something in her eyes—something he remembered from long ago.

"My name is Lawrence Arkos," he said. "I have come from America. I'm interested in talking to people who knew Nikos Vanos. Did you or anyone in this house know him?"

"Yes," said the woman, looking very surprised. Then she said, "Nikos was my son."

A man came to the door and asked, "Momma, what is it?"

"This young man," Mrs. Vanos began, "has come here to ask about Nikos."

The man looked hard at Larry. He was short, with a strong build. He looked about 50. "What do you want to know?" he asked.

"May I come in?" said Larry. "I can tell you better there."

"Yes, come in, please," said the woman.

The man and woman led him into a small sitting room. "Sit down, please," said the woman. The man left the room and soon returned with some wine. Pouring out a glass, he said, "I am George Vanos. Nikos was my brother." He handed Larry the glass, and Larry lifted it to his mouth. The dark red wine tasted strong.

"*Why* do you want to know about my son?" the woman asked.

"I—I knew him," said Larry.

Mrs. Vanos and George gave him strange looks. Larry knew he looked young. Maybe he looked too young to have known Nikos.

"*When* did you know my son?" Mrs. Vanos asked.

"I knew him when I was a child," Larry lied. He couldn't tell them what the old woman had said to him. If he did, they wouldn't tell him anything. "My family was staying in this village. It was before we left for America. We were here only a short time, but I remember Nikos well. He was very kind to me."

"What did you say your name was?" asked Mrs. Vanos.

"Arkos."

"I . . . don't remember your family," she said. "You—you seem so young to have known my son."

"I was only a child," said Larry. He felt very nervous now. His hand shook as he picked up the wineglass. He put it right down again.

"I've always remembered Nikos," he went on. "He used to play with me and tell me stories."

"My son was a very fine person, Mr. Arkos," said the woman. "But he is no longer with us. He has been dead 25 years now. He was killed in an accident."

"An accident?" said Larry. "What kind?"

"He was killed in a rock slide," said Mrs. Vanos. "Rocks came crashing down and killed him."

George Vanos spoke up. "A man named Grivas found the body. He and the chief of police brought it into town."

"Where did it happen?"

"On Grivas's land," said George. "On the other side of the mountain."

"Was Nikos the only one killed by the slide?"

"Yes, he was alone," said George.

"Why are you asking all these questions?" said the woman.

Larry decided to take a chance. "Mrs. Vanos, have you ever thought that perhaps Nikos's death was *not* an accident? Have you ever thought that perhaps your son was *murdered?*"

"I don't believe that," said George. He sounded very angry. He took a few steps toward Larry. Larry looked into his face and thought of what the old woman had said: *The murderer still lives.... You knew him ... believed in him.* Did Nikos perhaps believe too much in his own brother?

"Never, never have I thought of murder," said Mrs. Vanos. "Why do you ask such a question? Who are you, really? Who sent you here?"

"I *knew* your son," said Larry again.

"How could you know my son?" she said. "*What* do you know about my son?"

Larry's eyes went to the wall behind Mrs. Vanos. A picture hung there. Suddenly he remembered. Suddenly it all came back to him.

"I remember that when Nikos was young he stole a little money," said Larry. "I know where he put it. In a hole in the wall behind that picture."

Mrs. Vanos turned her head to the picture on

the wall. When she turned around again, her eyes were wide and filled with fear. She looked as though she couldn't believe what she was hearing.

"Later, you found it hidden there," said Larry. "You were very angry. You hit me—I mean you hit *him* very hard—so hard he cried. Then *you* cried, and you made him—"

"Stop!" Mrs. Vanos said. "How—*how* do

you—*know* this?" she asked. She looked at him with fear in her eyes. "*Who* are you?" she asked again. But her eyes told him that she already knew.

"Momma," said George. "What is it? What's wrong? What do you see in his face?"

"*No one* knows that story," Mrs. Vanos said. "No one . . . but Nikos and me. No one. I am sure of it. I made him say he would never tell anyone. How could *you* . . . ?"

"I have many dreams about Nikos," said Larry. "Today at his grave, I met an old woman in black. She lives in the stone house at the bottom of the hill. She told me that—"

Mrs. Vanos screamed.

"Aposta! The Evil One! *She* sent you here! The *devil* sent you here with these stories! That woman talks with the devil! That is how you know these things! You are with the devil!"

Suddenly she seemed to be losing her breath. She started to fall to the floor. George caught her at the last moment and slowly set her down. Quickly he bent over her and listened to her heart. He made sure she was still breathing.

Larry started to move toward her, but George held up his hand. "Stay back," he said.

"She'll be all right. She's a very nervous woman. She has spells. In a few minutes she'll be herself again."

Then George rose to his feet. He went and took a gun down from the wall behind him. He pointed the gun at Larry.

"Now you—leave this house," he said.

CHAPTER 4
A BAD DREAM

Larry walked slowly to the door. Opening it, he turned around to face George. George was still pointing the gun at him. Saying nothing, he turned and walked out into the night.

He shook as he walked past the old woman's stone house at the bottom of the hill. He found his car where he left it, got in, and drove back to the center of the village. There he found an inn where he could get a meal and a room for the night.

"Do you have a telephone?" he asked Zaimis, the man who ran the place. "I want to call America. I'll pay for the call now."

Zaimis showed Larry the phone. It was on a wall near the dining room. Larry made the call. He knew it was early morning in California. There were three or four rings before someone picked up the phone at the other end.

"Hello?" a tired voice said.

"Hello, Anne."

"Larry!" she said. "Where are you?"

"I'm still in Greece," he said. "I love you."

"I love you, too," she said. "When are you coming home?"

"Soon," he said.

"When is soon?" she asked.

"I'm not sure," he said. "But we've got to get married one of these days. Anne—I love you very much."

"Have . . . you found anything?" she asked. Larry had told her about his dreams. She knew why he had gone to Greece.

"Yes," he said. "I've found it—I've found Drokola."

For a few long moments, she said nothing. Her voice was shaking when she started to speak again.

"Darling—now I'm afraid—I'm very afraid for you," she said. "I. . . ."

"I'll be all right," he said. "I just have to—"

"Larry, please don't let anything happen to you. Please be careful!"

"Don't worry," he said. "I'll be careful. I just want to see this thing through."

"What have you found out so far?"

"I don't want to talk about it over the phone yet," he said. "I'll call you again in a couple of days. If you don't hear from me. . . ."

Suddenly, he could hear her crying.

"I'm so afraid, Larry," she said. "I'm so afraid I'll never see you again."

"Anne, please. I told you I'd be careful. I told you—"

"Last night I dreamed you were dead," she said. "You were buried somewhere under a pile of rocks. Larry. . . ."

Now Larry's hand shook as he held the phone. "Tell me about the dream," he said. "What else do you remember?"

Suddenly there was a click on the other end. Anne was gone. The phone had gone dead.

"Anne? Anne, are you there?"

There was no answer. Larry tried to call back, but he couldn't get through. He was told that the line to America had gone dead.

He held the phone in his hand for a long time. Finally, he put it down. Then he heard the sound of steps coming up behind him. Larry turned. Zaimis stood there holding some plates of food on a tray. "I have made this for you," he said. "You must be hungry."

Larry remembered he hadn't eaten since morning. He sat and ate, all the while feeling Zaimis's eyes on him. What was it? There was something about the man that bothered Larry.

After the meal, Larry went to his room. Feeling very tired, he got right into bed. He felt himself starting to fall asleep. Suddenly, he was awakened by a sharp, scratching sound. It sounded very near, as though someone or something were trying to get into the room. He sat up in bed and listened very carefully.

He heard a voice speaking his name. "Larry . . . Larry," it called. "Come to me . . . . Come to me now . . . . I need you." It sounded like a man's voice—a young man's. He got out of bed and looked out the window. Down below, the village street was dark and empty.

He came away from the window and sat back down on the bed. Then he heard the voice again. "Larry . . . Larry . . . I need you . . . . I need you." It sounded as though it were out in the street, moving around in the dark.

Larry got dressed and headed out of his room and down the stairs. The darkness made him move slowly. As he reached the ground floor of the inn, he heard the voice again.

"I'm out here, Larry . . . here in the night.

Come to my grave . . . . Come to my grave . . . . It's not too late."

Quickly, Larry opened the door of the inn and stepped out into the street. He saw something move in the shadows. It was a tall, dark form.

"Who is it?" he said. "Who's there?"

There was no answer. The dark shape moved through the night again. Now it seemed to be coming toward him.

A small light burned above a doorway across the narrow, empty street. Again Larry heard the sharp, scratching sound. The tall shape stepped out of the shadows and into the light. It was a young man. He was thin and dark-skinned.

"You know me," the man said.

"Who are you?" Larry asked.

"You know me," the young man said again.

"I don't," said Larry. "Who are you?"

"Don't you remember me?" the young man said. "We were so close. Have I been gone so long?"

"Who—" Larry started to ask again.

"You know me," the other said. "I'm Nikos. Look." Suddenly he turned his head and showed Larry the other side of his face. Most of it was eaten away. Larry felt sick. He wanted to run, but he couldn't. His legs wouldn't move. The young man started coming toward him again.

"Come to my grave," he said. "Come to the other side of the mountain. I died there. You died there. There you will see."

Coming close to Larry, he smiled. His broken teeth showed through the empty spaces in his face. Larry tried to shut his eyes, but he couldn't. The sight was horrible.

Now Nikos was upon him. His hand, soft and wet to the touch, reached out. It took hold of Larry's. Larry looked down. The hand was gray and coming apart in his own. Pieces of it were falling to the ground.

Nikos was laughing. "I died here," he shouted. "You died here. You stay here!" Reaching out with his other arm, he began to pull Larry toward him. Larry screamed.

Just then, he awoke in darkness. Another dream—one more horrible than the other—was over.

Larry got out of bed quickly and went to the window. As in the dream, the street below looked dark and empty.

He felt sick. Once again, he wanted to leave. I can still get out now, he thought. Before it's too late.

But he knew that it was already too late. He was in too far. He knew now that what he had said to Anne was true. He had to see this thing through to the end.

Then his heart jumped as he heard something moving on the steps outside his room. Afraid to move, he stood very still beside the open window. The steps came close. Then the door began to open. Larry got ready to strike.

CHAPTER **5**

CHIEF OF POLICE

It was Zaimis, the man who ran the inn.

"What do you want?" said Larry.

"I—I heard a scream," he said. "It came from up here."

"I was having a bad dream," said Larry. "I'm all right now."

Zaimis smiled. Without saying another word, he went back downstairs. When he was gone, Larry dressed. His hands shook. After a few minutes he walked slowly down the stairs and out into the street.

He stood in front of the door of the inn. It was almost morning. Over the tops of the houses across the street he could see the first soft light of the sun. Right away, he felt better.

He stepped out into the street and began to walk. In the distance he saw the sun rising from behind the mountain.

"It never changes. It's always the same," a voice said behind him.

Larry turned. Behind him was a short, heavy man of about 60. He wore a dark-green uniform.

"The sun never changes. This village never changes, either," said the man. "I am Stakos, the chief of police. You are Mr. Arkos. You have come here from America."

"Yes, that's right," said Larry. "But how did you—"

"Drokola is a very small place," said the chief. "I hear about everything that goes on here. Come with me. I'd like to talk to you. We're both up very early today."

Larry went with the chief to the place where he had his office. In the back was a small one-room jail.

Stakos poured a cup of coffee for Larry. "You have been asking questions about Nikos Vanos," he said. "Did you know him?"

"I—I knew him as a child," said Larry.

"What is it you want to know about Nikos Vanos?" Stakos asked him.

"I'd like to know something about his death," said Larry.

"I'm sure you already know the story," said

Stakos. But he went on to tell Larry the same story Mrs. Vanos had told him the night before. Nikos had been killed in a rock slide. His body had been found by Grivas, a landowner.

"Grivas called me," said the chief. "He asked me to come at once. The accident took place on his land."

"Was Nikos already dead when you got there?" Larry asked.

"Oh, yes," answered the chief. "I'm sure he died right away. His head was crushed. It was very sad. Grivas and I, together we carried his body back into town."

"Did you ever think that Nikos's death was not an accident? Did you check it out? Is it possible he was murdered?"

The chief gave Larry a strange look. Then he smiled, shaking his head from side to side. "No," he said, "I never thought so for a second. Such a strange question. Why, after all these years, should you ask such a question?"

"I've heard things," said Larry.

"What things?" said the chief.

Larry decided to trust Stakos and tell him everything. He told him about his dream, his search for Drokola. He told him about the old woman in the cemetery.

"A very strange story," said Stakos. "*Very* strange. But a dream is only a dream. And as for that old woman, that Aposta—she's a sick, evil, old woman. No one listens to her. If I were you, Mr. Arkos, I would go back to America. I'd forget all this talk of murder."

He looked hard at Larry. Then he added, "I'm telling you this for your own good."

"Perhaps you're right," said Larry.

"Of course I am," said Stakos, smiling again. "Believe me, these dreams of yours will stop the minute you stop thinking about them."

The chief led Larry to the door. "Now go home to America and enjoy yourself," he said. "You're young. Put all this behind you and have some fun."

"Perhaps I will," said Larry. "I feel better for having talked to you."

As the chief began to shut the door, Larry had a thought. "Could I ask you one more question?" he asked.

"Of course," said the chief.

"What was Nikos Vanos doing the day he was killed? *Why* was he on Grivas's land?"

The smile left the chief's face. "I don't know," he said. "I don't think that anyone does. I don't think it's important. It doesn't really matter."

"Probably it doesn't," said Larry. He thanked Stakos and left.

The first thing he saw as he walked away was the mountain behind the town. I can't leave yet, he thought to himself. Not until I go to the other side of the mountain. If there's anything to find out, I'll find it out there. I'm going to look for the place where Nikos died.

He walked back to the inn, got into his car, and headed for the mountain. He drove along the dirt road that went around it. In a few minutes he reached the other side. But the road went on only a little way further. Where it stopped a sign said "Danger—Falling Rocks."

Larry stopped the car and got out. He walked until he came to a high fence. A sign on the fence warned against going on. "This land belongs to P. Grivas," it said. "All others keep out."

Larry started to look for a way to get inside. After a while he found a place where the ground had fallen away from under the fence. He crawled under the fence and began to walk.

The land was uneven and covered with stones. Suddenly a great fear filled him. "I *know* this place," he said to himself. "Something very bad happened here. I know it."

Then, again, he had the feeling he was not alone. He felt that someone was watching him. Between two large stones he saw a dirt path that led off up the mountain. When he saw the path, his head began to hurt as it never had before.

"Here—it happened *here*," he said to himself.

Suddenly, he heard a rushing sound behind him. He turned, but not quickly enough. A large black dog was on him—going for his throat.

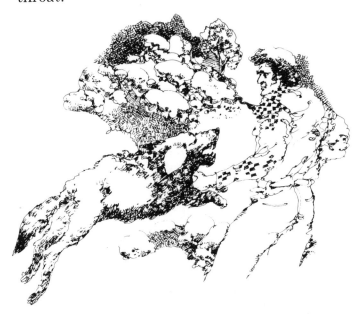

CHAPTER 6

CLOSED DOORS

Larry threw up his arm. The dog sunk its teeth into it and hung on, dragging him to the ground. Its teeth tore at his arm and drew blood. Any moment, the dog would be at his throat.

With his free arm, Larry reached for a stone that lay nearby. He grabbed it and raised it in the air, bringing it down on the animal's head. The dog howled, letting go of Larry's arm. Larry struck again, this time landing a blow on the side of its head. The animal fell to one side.

Behind Larry, a voice called, "Hold it! I'll shoot!"

Larry turned. Twenty feet away a tall, thin man was pointing a gun at him. Suddenly the dog was on its feet again. When the dog started to come at him again, Larry raised the stone.

"Narda! No! Come here!" the man shouted.

The animal turned slowly away from Larry and moved over to the man.

"Drop that stone," the man said to Larry. "Just drop it and you'll be all right."

Larry let it fall to the ground.

"Who are you?" said the man. "Are you Arkos, the American?"

"Yes," answered Larry.

"You should thank your luck you're alive, Mr. Arkos," said the man. He lowered his gun. "I am Paul Grivas. I own this land. Come to my house and I'll take care of your arm."

Larry walked with Grivas to a large white house that lay over the next hill. A two-color Rolls Royce was parked outside. A man held the front door open as Larry and Grivas went inside. Grivas hung up his gun beside several others on a wall.

The dog bites were not as deep as Larry had feared. Grivas cleaned off Larry's arm and put something on it. "You'll be all right," he said. "I hope my dog is as well as you are. You should learn to read signs, Mr. Arkos. You'll probably live longer if you do."

"I saw your sign," said Larry. "But I was looking for something."

"On my land?" asked Grivas. "What?"

"I was looking for the place where Nikos Vanos died."

"You found it," said Grivas. "Nikos died where my dog found you."

"May I ask you a question, Mr. Grivas?"

Grivas smiled. "About Nikos Vanos?"

"Yes," said Larry. "What was he doing on your land the day he was killed?"

"I don't know," said Grivas. "It was a long time ago."

"Please tell me what you remember," Larry said.

Grivas stood up. "There's little to tell, Mr. Arkos," he said. "There was a rock slide. I found the body and saw that Nikos was dead. That was all. Now, Mr. Arkos, you must leave. I'm a busy person, and I don't have any more time to waste on this. You know, you're a strange young man."

"Why do you say that?" said Larry.

"Most people are afraid of me. They do what I tell them to do. I have a lot of power. But *you* don't seem to be afraid of anything. That's too bad for you, Mr. Arkos. You might get yourself in trouble. You should be more careful."

"You sound as if you're trying to frighten me," said Larry.

"I'm telling you to leave Drokola very soon. Good-bye, Mr. Arkos," said Grivas. Without another word he turned and left the room.

One of Grivas's men walked Larry back to his car. Larry saw that the man carried a gun. Larry got into the car and drove back to town.

Zaimis was waiting for him as he came to the door of the inn. "I must ask you to leave, Mr.

Arkos," said Zaimis. "You can no longer stay here."

"What do you mean?" said Larry.

"We no longer have room," said Zaimis.

Larry got his things and handed over the key. As he headed for the door, he thought of what Grivas had said: *Most people are afraid of me. They do what I tell them to do.* Stepping out into the street, he saw a group of people looking at him. Their faces were not friendly.

Larry got in his car and headed for the road that led to the Vanos place. He wanted to try to talk to Nikos's mother and his brother George one more time. When he got to the house, he got out of the car and headed up the front steps. The front door opened. George came out.

"What do *you* want?" he said.

"I have to talk to you, George," said Larry.

"Go away," said George. "You've caused enough trouble here." George turned and started back into the house.

"Wait!" said Larry. "I have to ask you one question. If you answer it I'll go away and leave you alone."

George said nothing for a few moments. He looked at Larry.

"What was Nikos doing the day he was killed?" Larry asked. "What was he doing on Grivas's land?"

"I don't know," said George.

"You *do* know," said Larry. "Tell me."

Again George didn't speak. Standing there, he seemed to be making up his mind about something.

"All right," George said finally. "I'll tell you."

CHAPTER **7**

ANSWERS

"He went to look for the gold," said George.

"What gold?" asked Larry.

"The gold the Germans buried," said George. "During the war a patrol of Germans passed through Drokola. It was believed they were carrying a lot of gold they stole from the state bank at Volos. Many people believed they buried it in the mountain behind the town."

"It was never found?"

"No. For years after the war, people looked for it. That was what Nikos was doing the day he was killed—looking for the buried gold."

"Maybe he found it," said Larry. "Maybe that was why he was killed."

George started to go back into the house. "I told you it was an *accident*."

"Why are you so sure it was an accident?" Larry called after him. "Who told you?"

"The police chief, Stakos, and Grivas," he answered. "They both knew. They—"

"Tell me," said Larry. "Did you see the body? Did you see it for *yourself?*"

George stopped. He stood for what seemed a long time without speaking. Then he went on talking.

"They told me there was nothing to see," he said in a low voice. It was all coming back to him. "Stakos—the chief—he said Nikos's head was crushed. He said it was better we didn't look. So Nikos was put in a closed coffin. We never saw him."

"Who put him in the coffin? Who took care of the funeral?"

"Stakos," said George, looking away. "He did that in those days. He was also the undertaker here. In a small town, a person must do many things to stay alive."

Without another word, George turned and went back into the house.

Larry watched him go. Then, turning, he looked down the hill and saw the little stone hut in which the old woman, Aposta, lived. Beyond it was the cemetery.

The answer may still be in Nikos's coffin,

Larry thought. Tonight, I'll see Nikos's body for myself.

Getting back into his car, he headed for town. I'll let them think I'm leaving, he thought to himself. He drove through the town and then on to the main road that led out of it. He drove for an hour and then stopped in another town. He went into a store and bought a shovel.

"Is there anything else you need?" asked the woman who ran the store.

"Yes, I want to buy a gun," said Larry.

"Doing some hunting?" asked the woman.

Larry didn't answer. He bought a fast-firing hunting gun. He put it and the shovel in the back of his car. Then he drove off.

It was dark as he came near Drokola. But he didn't want to drive through the town. He took another road that went around the town and led to the cemetery.

He drove slowly and without lights. Finally, near the cemetery, he stopped and parked off the road. He got out and took the shovel and gun out of the back. Then he began to walk.

He walked toward the stone house where the old woman, Aposta, lived. He saw that the front door was open, blowing back and forth in the

wind. He wanted to go on, but he had a feeling that something was wrong inside the house. From inside he could hear a kind of high, sharp, singing sound. A chill went through him.

Slowly he went up to the front door. Inside, the light was low. But he could see across the room. He could see Aposta's body on a bed on the floor. She wasn't moving. She looked very stiff and white and dead.

Suddenly she spoke in a high, sharp voice. "Nikos—come to me—come to me."

Larry went in. He put down the gun and shovel and walked across the room to her. She opened her eyes when he came near. He sat down on the floor beside her.

"My son," she said. "I am . . . waiting . . . for death. I know it is coming for me. . . . I can feel it out there in the night. . . . I have waited for you to come back. . . . I cannot die in peace . . . until you come . . . until you find the answer. . . ."

She reached out and put her thin fingers to his face. "Once you were mine," she said. "You were Nikos . . . my son. . . . You were my baby. . . . Then they came and took you away from me. . . . They said I was bad . . . bad for you. . . . Now you have come back."

Now Larry knew. The old woman had been Nikos's true mother.

"I knew that . . . in some place far away . . . you were born again. . . . When I felt death coming close . . . I sent for you . . . in my thoughts."

Now he knew. *She* had sent the strange dreams that had brought him here.

She looked up into his eyes. "You lived here," she said. "You died here. You stay here . . . until you know. . . ."

Behind him, Larry heard a sound. He turned. It was only the front door, banging in the wind. Turning back to her, he said, "Tonight I'll know, Mother. Then I'll come back to you."

"Yes, you go now," she said. Her fingers slipped from his face as her eyes closed again. Getting up from beside her, Larry picked up the shovel and gun. As he went out the door, he turned and looked back at her one last time.

"Go now," she said. "It is time."

He went out the door and started to walk. All was still and black. There was no moon, no sound from anywhere.

When he got to the cemetery, he opened the gate. It made a loud, squeaking sound as it swung slowly open. He made his way with care. At Nikos's grave, he began to dig.

CHAPTER 8

IN THE GRAVE

He dug for almost an hour. Finally, his shovel struck something that felt like wood. It was Nikos's coffin.

Suddenly he heard a sound—like someone opening the cemetery gate. He was standing on the coffin, the top of the grave just above his head. He pulled himself up and sat on the edge of the grave. He saw nothing.

A full minute went by. Still he saw nothing, heard nothing. Then he dropped back down onto the coffin, placing the gun beside it. His heart pounded in his ears as he dug the last bit of dirt away from the sides. The wood had gone bad in places, but most of it was still there.

Taking a deep breath, he reached down and pulled the lid open. Inside he saw a pile of bones. Then he saw a skull. It was badly cracked in two places. He picked up the skull and turned it around. In back was a small, round hole. This could mean only one thing: Someone had killed Nikos by firing a bullet into the back of his head.

Now everything made sense. The dreams. The old woman's talk of murder. He had not come to this place for nothing.

Then he heard a sound. It was very near, almost on top of him. As he turned to reach for the gun, a very bright light hit his eyes. For a moment, he couldn't see.

"Hold it right there, Mr. Arkos. I'll shoot to kill."

The voice belonged to Stakos, the police chief. Larry moved toward his gun again.

"I'll kill you, Mr. Arkos. Don't reach for it."

Another voice said, "Let's bring him up." Larry knew that voice, too. It was Grivas talking. "Come up, Mr. Arkos," he said.

Larry climbed out of the grave. He saw two men standing there. Like the two who chased him in the dream. Both were dressed in black.

"Get the shovel," Grivas said to the police chief. He held a gun and a light on Larry as the chief slid down into the grave. In a few moments, Stakos was back up with the shovel and

the gun. "Give the shovel to him," Grivas said
to Stakos. Stakos handed it to Larry.

"Now fill it in," said Grivas.

Grivas and Stakos stood about ten feet from
Larry and from each other. Both held lights
and guns on Larry as he began throwing dirt
back into the grave.

"Which one of you killed him?" Larry asked.

"Does it matter?" said Grivas.

"It was you, wasn't it?" he said to Grivas.

"I didn't want to," said Grivas. "Just like I don't want to kill you."

"But you will," said Larry.

Grivas said nothing.

Larry was almost finished when he heard a sound from the road. Turning toward the sound, Grivas and Stakos switched off their lights. Someone was walking on the road near the cemetery. In the sudden darkness, Larry saw his chance. They'll kill me anyway, he thought. I have nothing to lose. He dropped the shovel and took off running.

"Stop!" Stakos cried. He fired his gun in the dark. The bullet went past Larry. He kept going and reached the fence, but he couldn't find the gate. As he started to climb the fence, he could hear Grivas and the chief running up behind him. A moment later, something hit him from behind. Everything went black.

When Larry came to, Grivas and Stakos were dragging him out the front gate. As they came to the road, someone stepped out of the darkness. It was George Vanos.

"I heard a shot," said George. "What's wrong?"

"It's nothing, George," said Stakos. "Go home. We'll take care of this."

George stayed a few moments. He didn't seem to know what to do. Finally he started to walk away. Then he stopped. He turned and came back. "I want to know," he said in a quiet voice.

"Then you'd better come with us," said Grivas, pointing his gun at him.

The four men walked up the road to Larry's car. "We were driving by to check the cemetery. When we found your car, we knew where you'd be," said Stakos. "Get in." Larry got in the back seat with Grivas. George rode up front with Stakos.

As Stakos started up the car, Grivas knocked George out with his gun. "Just in case," Grivas said to Larry. "I wouldn't want him to get any ideas."

Then he put the mouth of his gun to Larry's head. "I wouldn't want you to get any ideas, either," he said.

They took off. Within a few minutes, Larry could see that they were headed for the other side of the mountain.

CHAPTER **9**

THE SLIDE

"How will you kill us?" Larry asked Grivas. "Will it be another *accident?* Another *rock slide?*"

Grivas didn't answer right away. "It will be an accident," he said finally.

"Why did you kill Nikos?" Larry asked.

"It doesn't matter," said Grivas.

"I want to know," said Larry. "You have nothing to lose. You're going to kill me. Was it because he found the gold?"

"As you like," said Grivas. "Because he found the gold. Yes."

"Until then only *you* knew where the gold was?"

"I was with the Germans the day they buried it high up the side of the mountain," Grivas answered.

"You were with the Germans?"

"I was helping them," said Grivas. "For a time it looked as though they would win the war."

"Why did you leave the gold on your land? Why didn't you move it?"

"I couldn't," said Grivas. "Not without help. And I wasn't willing to share it with anyone else. So I sold it off a little at a time, outside the country. It's all gone now."

"But before that happened Nikos found it?"

"Yes," said Grivas. "Like a fool he came and told me how he had found it on my land. I asked him to show me the place."

"That was when you shot him?"

"Of course," said Grivas. "I couldn't let him live. The gold didn't belong to me. I would have gone to jail. After I shot him, I called the chief of police. I knew I could pay him with part of the gold to help me. Together we decided to make Nikos's death look like an accident."

The car picked up speed. Larry looked out the window and saw they were coming to the other side of the mountain.

"There really *was* a rock slide," said Grivas. "But it happened after Nikos died. Stakos and I *made* one happen. There are often rock slides up here. They're easy enough to start. A very loud noise will often do the trick. So we put Nikos at the bottom of the mountain. Then we shot our guns. The noise started a rock slide that covered his body."

Stakos stopped the car. "This is it," he said, turning to Grivas.

"Good," said Grivas. "Tie them up," he said to the chief.

Stakos moved Larry into the front seat of the car beside George. George now sat in the driver's seat, still knocked out. Stakos tied both men's arms behind their backs. Then he tied their legs. He placed George's foot on the gas pedal and tied it down. Finally, he placed a large stone under the foot brake.

"Do you want to know what's going to happen?" said Grivas. "Your car is going to go off the side of the mountain. The road is not very wide, and the turns are very sharp up here. It's a big drop. You won't suffer for very long."

"And you and Stakos will find our bodies?"

"Certainly," said Grivas. "Of course we'll take the ropes off your bodies before we tell anyone about the accident."

"Come on, let's go," said Stakos. "Let's get this over with."

"Good-bye, Mr. Arkos," said Grivas, turning away.

Stakos reached in and turned on the car's motor. When he moved the hand brake down, the car took off. It picked up speed as it headed down the mountain. The first sharp turn was less than 300 yards away. George had fallen forward against the wheel. Larry knew that his only chance was to reach the hand brake.

Pulling his body around, he fell back against the brake. He reached around and down with his fingers. The bend in the road was coming up soon. And the car was moving even faster now.

He felt his fingers touch the hand brake. Then the car hit a bump, and he lost hold of the brake. He made one last quick grab and pulled as hard as he could.

The car skidded about 30 feet, hit a large rock, and turned over. When the car stopped rocking, Larry looked out the window. All he could see was darkness. They were still on the road—upside down but alive.

Twisting his body around, Larry felt for the door. The voices of Stakos and Grivas came

closer as they ran up the road toward the car. Then, from above, came a terrible sound—a great rumbling noise.

The noise grew louder and louder. Finally, Larry's hand found the door handle. He pulled on it, but he couldn't get it open. Suddenly, something crashed down on the overturned car. It was a rock. Then another one hit the car. Then a big rock smashed in the side window.

It was a rock slide, started by the noise of the crash. Big rocks were falling all around them.

It lasted less than a minute, then it was over. Larry pushed against the car door. It finally came open. Slowly he climbed out. The dust in the air made him cough. The car was half buried by rocks, but being inside it had saved Larry and George's lives.

Larry looked through the darkness at the road behind him. There was no sign of either Grivas or Stakos.

He found a piece of broken window and used it to slowly cut away his ropes. Then he pulled George out of the car. George was just beginning to come to. Together they made their way back down the mountain road and into the town.

A few hours later, the bodies of Grivas and the chief were found. They had been buried in the slide only 100 yards from the wrecked car. It was finally over. All over. Larry had seen it through, after all.

The next afternoon, Larry found himself standing with George in front of Nikos's grave. Nearby, men were digging three new graves. Two were for Grivas and Stakos. The third was for Aposta, who had died during the night.

"Do you think she knew how it all turned out?" asked George.

"I'm sure she did," answered Larry. "She couldn't die until Nikos's death had been paid for. I'm sure she died right after the rock slide."

"How soon will you go back to America?" George asked him.

"In a day or two," answered Larry. "First I want to see the old woman buried. After all, she was my mother in another life."

"Do you really believe that?" George asked him.

"Yes," said Larry. He looked down at Nikos's grave. "I believe I was once Nikos Vanos. I was once your brother. I lived here. I died here. Last night, you and I were brothers again. Thank you for trying to help me."

"I was always afraid to try to find out the real truth about Nikos's death," said George. "The whole town was afraid of Grivas."

"You weren't afraid last night," said Larry.

"You were putting yourself in great danger to find out the truth," said George. "Nikos was my brother. I had to help you."

"And I had to find out the truth," said Larry

as he and George began to walk to the cemetery gate. "I knew if I didn't I'd dream about this grave every night for the rest of my life."

George smiled. "Well, you should sleep well tonight."

"Yes," said Larry. "I think I will sleep very well from now on."